The Circus Mystery
A WOODLAND MYSTERY
By Irene Schultz

Wright Group
McGraw-Hill

To Julie and all my wonderful school children

The Circus Mystery
Text copyright © Irene Schultz
Illustrations copyright © Wright Group/McGraw-Hill
Cover and cameo illustrations by Taylor Bruce
Interior illustrations by Meredith Yasui, Tom Boatman,
and Charles Solway
Map illustration by Alicia Kramer

Woodland Mysteries® is a registered trademark of
Wright Group/McGraw-Hill.

Wright Group/McGraw-Hill
19201 120th Avenue NE, Suite 100
Bothell, WA 98011
www.WrightGroup.com

Printed in the United States of America

10 9 8

ISBN: 0-7802-7244-7
ISBN: 0-7802-7942-5 (6-pack)

What family solves mysteries...has adventures all over the world...and loves oatmeal cookies?

It's the Woodlanders!

Sammy Westburg (10 years old)
His sister Kathy Westburg (13)
His brother Bill Westburg (14)
His best friend Dave Briggs (16)
His best grown-up friend Mrs. Tandy
And Mop, their little dog!

The children all lost their parents, but with Mrs. Tandy have made their own family.

Why are they called the Woodlanders? Because they live in a big house in the Bluff Lake woods. On Woodland Street!

Together they find fun, mystery, and adventure. What are they up to now?

Read on!

Meet the Woodlanders!

Sammy Westburg
Sammy is a ten-year-old wonder! He's big for his fifth-grade class, and big-mouthed, too. He has wild hair and makes awful spider faces. Even so, you can't help liking him.

Bill Westburg
Bill, fourteen, is friendly and strong, and only one inch taller than his brother Sammy. He loves Sammy, but pokes him to make him be quiet! He's in junior high.

Kathy Westburg
Kathy, thirteen, is small, shy, and smart. She wants to be a doctor some day! She loves to be with Dave, and her brothers kid her about it. She's in junior high, too.

Dave Briggs

Dave, sixteen, is tall and blond. He can't walk, so he uses a wheelchair and drives a special car. He likes coaching high-school sports, solving mysteries, and reading. And Kathy!

Mrs. Tandy

Sometimes the kids call her Mrs. T. She's Becky Tandy, their tall, thin, caring friend. She's always ready for a new adventure, and for making cookies!

Mop

Mop is the family's little tan dog. Sometimes they have to leave him behind with friends. But he'd much rather be running after Sammy.

Table of Contents

Chapter		Page
1	Peanut Hair	1
2	The Baby Gorilla	9
3	The Milking Barn	19
4	Run for Your Life!	27
5	The Stolen Animals	37
6	The Blue Truck	45
7	A Good Guy or a Crook?	53
8	Surprise Company	61
9	The Stranger	73
10	The Five New Clowns	85
11	The Dark Circus Tent	95
12	The Clowns at Work	101
13	The Show's Over!	111

Chapter 1:
Peanut Hair

Ten-year-old Sammy Westburg shouted,
"Hey! Help! Something just landed in
my hair!"

He and his fourteen-year-old brother

Bill stood in front of a cage at the Parker Zoo Farm.

Bill picked a peanut out of Sammy's hair. He said, "This is the first time I've seen a chimp throw a peanut at a VISITOR!

"It must like you. Or maybe it thinks you look hungry."

He looked at his chubby brother. "No, I doubt that!"

Sammy grabbed the peanut from Bill. He stuffed it inside his brother's shirt and ran off toward another cage.

A minute later, Sammy shouted, "Hey, look at THIS guy! What IS it?"

He was pointing at an animal with a very long nose. He said, "It's nosing around in there like a pig. But it's got fur, and it's not a pig."

He stuffed a handful of popcorn into his mouth.

2

Bill said, "Not a popcorn pig, any-way."

Sammy made his worst poison-spider face at Bill.

Their sixteen-year-old friend Dave Briggs was farther down the path in his wheelchair.

He called back to them, "That's an anteater! But come over here and look at this little pygmy elephant!"

Bill said, "About as little as a station wagon! But he does look small next to the other elephants. That's probably why they call him Baby."

His thirteen-year-old sister Kathy smiled and said, "I wish we could keep a pygmy elephant in our woods in Bluff Lake."

Mrs. Tandy laughed. "That would go over big with the neighbors!"

∎   ∎   ∎

The five Woodlanders walked along and talked.

They didn't see the gray-haired man with a cane who was walking behind them.

He was looking at the animals. But he was also trying to hear what they were saying.

∎   ∎   ∎

Dave said, "The sign over there said

that little elephant is new here at the zoo. Coco the chimpanzee, too."

Sammy said, "That chimp is new? So maybe he doesn't know any better than to throw peanuts at visitors!"

Bill said, "Did it say where the zoo got them, Dave?"

Dave said, "They bought them from a circus. I guess the zoo needed a chimpanzee, and the circus needed money.

"And it said the pygmy elephant is pretty old. He wasn't strong enough to travel with the circus anymore.

"But Mr. Lopez paid a lot for him anyway. Those elephants are really rare."

Kathy said, "Who's Mr. Lopez?"

Mrs. Tandy said, "He owns this whole zoo farm."

Sammy said, "I bet Baby and Coco will miss the circus ... but WE better not

5

miss it! I can't wait until it comes to Bluff Lake tomorrow night!

"I think I'm going to be a circus clown when I grow up!"

Bill said, "That's the perfect job for you. You can let your hair get even wilder than it is now. And you can wear peanuts in it!"

He danced around Sammy. "You can be Peanut Hair, the Nutty Clown!" he teased.

Sammy said, "And in a minute YOU'RE going to be his brother clown, Bloody-Nose Bill!"

Sammy ran to catch him.

Mrs. Tandy, Dave, and Kathy headed for the seal pool.

Kathy called, "Hey, look, Sammy! You can get fish from this machine ... to feed the seals!"

Sammy ran over. "Come on, Kathy.

You can't buy a wet fish from a machine! YUCK! It would rot in there. It's not like a candy bar!"

Kathy said, "You can, too! Read the sign!"

The sign looked like this:

Please don't make the seals sick with the wrong food. Buy them what they like.

Fresh cold fish.
10¢ each

Dave said, "Here, I've got five dimes."
He dropped them into the machine.
Out came five icy-cold fish.
Sammy held his fish up by its tail.

Two seals at the side of the pool began to clap their flippers together.

Sammy threw the fish into the water and both seals dived in.

Sammy shouted, "Quick, everybody! Throw in your fish before the seals get into a fight over mine!"

Four more fish flew through the air and landed in the pool.

The Woodlanders watched the seals dive for them.

■   ■   ■

And the man with the cane watched the Woodlanders.

Chapter 2:
The Baby Gorilla

In a few minutes Sammy said, "I'm so hungry I'm getting weak.

"I'll eat a raw fish myself if you don't give me some of our food!"

Dave laughed. He said, "No problem, Sammy. There are some picnic tables right here."

He lifted a paper bag from the side pocket of his wheelchair. There were boiled eggs, sliced chicken, and apples inside.

The old man with the cane sat down at a table behind them and opened his newspaper.

At another table near them, two zoo workers sat sipping coffee and talking.

The young man said, "I've been in charge of this place for three years, Jane, and I've never seen anything like this happen."

The young woman said, "I haven't either, Harry. It's a mystery all right!"

The Woodlanders kept on eating, but they stopped talking.

They loved mysteries and were all

listening in.

Harry said, "That new guy we just hired is no prize. I think he's sneaky and lazy.

"I'm pretty sure he's behind some of our problems."

Jane said, "Like what?"

Harry said, "Well, the other day when big old Silver almost killed the baby gorilla?

"My guess is, the new guy wasn't feeding Silver enough.

"I think the gorilla went crazy from hunger ... he's always been so gentle before this."

Jane said, "I wish I knew how the baby was able to get away from him.

"She must have somehow squeezed out between the bars of the gorilla cage ... and found her way to a safe, empty cage.

"And with a broken arm, too.
"Poor dear. It IS a mystery."

She picked up a white bundle from a
box next to her and held a baby bottle
to it.

She said, "You dear little thing." The
next minute a hairy little brown arm
reached out and took hold of the bottle.

Sammy cried, "Hey! You have a baby
gorilla right there with you! This is even

better than the circus. I LOVE this!"

Jane smiled. "I'm the vet for the zoo animals. Would you like to help feed Peewee here?

"You could hold her bottle while I hold her."

Sammy said, "SURE! And let Kathy have a turn, too, OK? She wants to be a doctor, and she's very gentle."

Sammy held the bottle for Peewee.

Bill said, "How about letting me take a turn? I know a lot about feeding little animals. I used to feed Sammy all the time."

Sammy said, "Very funny, very funny. But this is MY gorilla baby. So hands off!"

Jane laughed. "All of you can try it for a while, if you want. Sammy, show them just how you're doing it. It's perfect."

So Kathy had a try, then Bill, then Dave, then Mrs. Tandy!

Soon Jane and Harry were telling them all about another mystery at the zoo farm.

Harry said, "Something really strange happened last night.

"One of our prize cows was going to have a calf.

"But the calf was born before we expected it, in the middle of the night. We weren't there to help."

Kathy said, "Oh, no! Is the calf OK?"

Harry said, "Yes. That's what's so strange. Somebody must have gone into the field and helped the calf and its mother.

"And after that, whoever it was put them both into the barn."

Jane said, "And then there's ANOTHER mystery! Someone got into the baby-animal house at mid night last week.

"They un-locked the cages of two rare animals.

"But then the lights flashed on and off in there ... so one of the guards looked in. He found the un-locked cages."

Harry said, "Looks like someone planned to steal some animals from the zoo that night. And someone ELSE

15

flashed the lights and stopped him."

■　　■　　■

The man with the cane was still sitting at the next table.　His eyelids were almost shut, as if he were half-asleep. But he was listening to every word.

■　　■　　■

Dave said, "Look, Harry.　I'm Dave Briggs.　These are my best friends ... Kathy, Bill, and Sammy Westburg, and Mrs. Tandy.

"We live in Bluff Lake."

He went on.　"And, we are really good at solving mysteries.　If we can help you, let us know.

"Here's our phone number."

Dave handed Harry a piece of paper.

Then Bill said, "Hey, it's nearly time to go see the milking.　We better head over to the barn."

Mrs. Tandy said, "It was a thrill to feed Peewee. Thanks so much!"

Sammy said, "And remember, if you need a real expert to feed her again, call on me.

"I'm a lot better at it than Bill."

Then Sammy added, "And listen, Harry, I've been thinking. You're missing some hair on top of your head, but Peewee is COVERED with hair.

"SHE'S the one who should be called Harry!"

Bill and Kathy poked Sammy, but Harry wasn't mad. He and Jane laughed.

Then Sammy leaned over to take a last look at Peewee. Suddenly a skinny brown arm shot up, and a little hand grabbed his ear.

"Ouch!" Sammy yelped in surprise.

Jane laughed and opened the gorilla's

little fingers. She said, "She doesn't want to let you go!"

The Woodlanders waved good-bye and headed for the milking barn.

■　　■　　■

The old man got up from the table. He took out a pencil and paper and wrote, "Dave Briggs, Kathy, Sammy, Bill Westburg. Mrs. Tandy. Bluff Lake."

Then he picked up his cane and walked slowly after them to the milking barn.

Chapter 3:
The Milking Barn

The milking barn was huge.

The Woodlanders went in the front door.

They looked at the cows through a big
glass wall.

Sammy said, "I wanted to pet the cows! Why are they all kept apart from the visitors?

"And how come everything in there is made of plastic and steel?"

Kathy said, "I don't know. I always expect straw and wood in a barn. And little milking stools."

Bill said, "Plastic is probably a lot easier to keep clean. And the glass wall keeps the cows from getting scared by the visitors."

Dave said, "And the visitors from getting scared by the cows!"

Mrs. Tandy laughed. "My word! When I milked cows as a child I never DREAMED there would be milking machines someday!"

Sammy said, "Well, milking by hand is still better."

He added, "I like that brown cow over

there. And I think she likes me. She keeps looking at me."

Kathy said, "I like the little brown-and-white one on this end."

Dave said, "Uh-oh. They're closing the barn to visitors now. I guess it's time to head home."

As they were leaving the barn, Harry walked by.

He said, "Well? How did you like it in there?"

Sammy said, "It was great, but we like hand-milking better."

Harry said, "Hmm... you ALL know how to milk? Tell you what. Come with me. We have some cows who need you."

He took them into the big part of the milking barn.

He sat Mrs. Tandy, Sammy, Bill, and Kathy down on some milking stools. Dave got ready to milk from his wheelchair.

In a minute the Woodlanders were all listening to the sound of milk shooting into their pails.

Sammy said, "I'm so good at this! Maybe when I grow up I'll be a farmer instead of a clown."

Bill said, "Harry, now if your power ever goes out, you'll know five hand-milkers who can help you."

Harry laughed. "I'll remember that!"

Dave said, "Thanks for letting us stay late."

Kathy added, "This was a wonderful day."

■ ■ ■

As they drove off, they didn't see the old man throw his cane into a blue truck. He started it up and followed them to Bluff Lake.

■ ■ ■

When they got home, their little dog Mop kept jumping up to lick their hands.

Sammy said, "Holy cats! Is Mop glad to see us! He HATES to be stuck at home with just a rabbit to keep him company. Hi, Moppy."

Just then Bill cried, "Good grief! Look!"

They all ran into the dining room.

Bill said, "Jumper's missing from her box AGAIN. Start the rabbit hunt, guys."

Sammy said, "That rotten rabbit. She's gotten out about ten times this week."

Bill added, "Every time you put her into a taller box, she just learns to jump higher."

After a few minutes Kathy called, "Here she is! She was under Sammy's bed!"

Dave said, "Well, now at least we can get our homework out of the way."

By 10:00 their homework for the rest of the four-day weekend was done.

Sammy said, "I LOVE school holidays. I'm just going to stay in bed in the morning and read old comic books. I'm getting up LATE."

Mrs. Tandy said, "We could roast hot dogs for breakfast tomorrow ... in the clubhouse fireplace!"

Kathy said, "Perfect. Then we can work on a new box for Jumper. If we don't, our house will smell like the zoo farm!"

They went to bed at last. They turned out the lights.

■　　■　　■

They didn't know that for an hour after that a stranger walked back and forth in their woods in the moonlight.

Chapter 4:
Run for Your Life!

Sammy didn't sleep as late as he had planned Friday morning.

He heard a noise.

It was a very soft noise, but it woke

him up at 6:00.

Then something landed on his legs and ran up to his chest. Mop was standing on him, licking his face.

Sammy yelled, "What in the world is going on here!"

He looked at the floor. There was Jumper. Mop had been running away from the rabbit!

Sammy moaned, "Somebody save me. Why did I ever say YES when that kid asked me if I wanted a rabbit?"

By then Kathy had come to his door. She said, "What's wrong, Sammy? Was that you moaning?"

She saw Jumper. She said, "So THAT'S the trouble! She sure seems to love your room and hate her box.

"I guess you'll have to buy a real cage for her after all."

She picked Jumper up and took her

back to her box.

Sammy cried, "That settles it!" He hugged Mop against him to keep warm. He followed Kathy and went right past her into the kitchen.

He made toast for them both.

He said, "Sit down, Kathy. I have something important to tell you ... I'm giving Jumper away."

Kathy said, "But you tried to do that last weekend. Your friends' parents all said no."

Sammy said, "Don't worry. I have a whole new plan ... you'll see."

He made more toast. The good toast smell brought Bill into the kitchen.

Then Sammy bumped some jars together as he took jelly and eggs out of the refrigerator.

Mrs. Tandy heard that, and padded out in her slippers.

She said, "I like this new breakfast plan, but isn't six o'clock a little early?"

Sammy said, "I woke up early this morning with the STRONG feeling I should go back to the zoo farm today."

He got out a frying pan and started making eggs.

Kathy gave him a look. She said, "That's funny. I thought you woke up with the STRONG feeling there was a dog on top of you."

Sammy said, "Let's just say I'd like to go back, that's all."

Bill said, "Well, that's not a bad idea ... Peanut Hair, the Nutty Clown."

Sammy stuck out his tongue.

Then Dave wheeled into the kitchen.

He said, "Hey, you guys. What happened to the sleeping-late plan?

"And what's this about going back to the zoo?"

He helped himself to some toast.

Everybody sat down for breakfast.

Mrs. Tandy said, "Sammy and Bill want to. And I'd sort of like it, too. I smell a mystery out there."

Dave said, "Then let's do it!"

Kathy said, "They open at nine o'clock. Let's be ready to leave around eight thirty, OK?"

They met in the garage at 8:30.

Mrs. Tandy had a big shopping bag full of snacks.

Sammy had a shopping bag, too. Its handles were tied together.

Bill asked, "What are you taking,

Sammy?   A lunch all for yourself?"

Sammy said, "This is a SECRET bag. No one will know what's in it until the magic moment."

Mrs. Tandy called, "Want to put it in the trunk with mine?"

Sammy shouted, "No, thanks!" He set the bag on the car floor between his feet.

All of a sudden the secret bag gave a little jump forward and fell on its side.

A soft black nose poked out of the bag.

Bill said, "Well, well.   Some secret. You've got Jumper with you."

Kathy said, "How come you're taking her to the zoo?   You said you were giving her away."

Sammy just said, "I have my reasons. Maybe she'd like a little ride in the car, OK? Let's go."

As they drove away, Dave pressed the

button to close the garage door.

He said, "By the way, the garage door was open this morning.

"Didn't I close it last night?"

No one remembered for sure.

Mrs. Tandy said, "I think you must have. You always do."

Bill asked, "Then who'd have opened it? Maybe we should report this to Chief Hemster before we leave town ... just to be safe."

Dave said, "That's a good idea. I'll stop at the police station on the way."

Sammy said, "Mrs. T. will sure love that. Maybe Chief Hemster will even follow her to the zoo!"

He loved to tease Mrs. Tandy about their friend the police chief.

When they told Chief Hemster about the garage door, he said, "I'll have an officer drive by your house today to keep an eye on things.

"Where are you headed, anyway? I'm off-duty from now until the circus tonight!"

It worked out just the way Sammy had said. The chief followed them to the zoo!

They met in the zoo farm's parking lot.

Before anyone could say anything, Sammy said, "Let's split up and meet later." And off he ran with his shopping bag.

In just five minutes he was back.

His shopping bag was gone.

Bill said, "Sammy! You forgot Jumper somewhere?"

But Sammy just said, "Follow me." He led them over to a huge outdoor pen.

There were big, fancy birds and dozens of gray rabbits in it.

Hopping around with them was one black rabbit.

Bill shouted, "It's Jumper! Sammy, I can't BELIEVE you put her in there!"

Sammy walked to a corner of the pen.

He said, "Why not? Yesterday I saw this fence was sort of broken. So today I pushed on it a little, and Jumper ran inside."

Kathy said, "I get it. You didn't give Jumper away. You let Jumper give herself away."

Dave said, "We should ask Jane and

Harry if it's OK to have Jumper in there."

But just then they heard someone shouting, near the lion house.

"GET INSIDE! RUN FOR YOUR LIFE! A LION'S OUT! A LION'S LOOSE! RUN FOR YOUR LIFE!"

Sammy grabbed Bill's arm.

Dave yelled, "Come on! Into the bird house!"

They all grabbed Dave's chair and pushed him up the ramp and inside.

Chief Hemster got the other visitors into the bird house.

Kathy slammed the door hard, just in time.

A moment later they saw a huge lion staring at them through the glass at the top of the door.

They all held their breath as the lion clawed at the door.

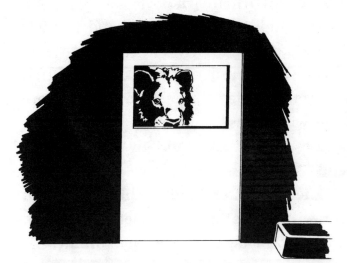

Chapter 5:
The Stolen Animals

Kathy was shaking all over. She said, "What if it p-pushes its w-way in?"

Dave said, "It can't. That's special glass. And the door opens out. Don't worry, Kathy."

The lion gave an awful roar and jumped against the glass.

But suddenly it turned ... and fell flat on the steps.

The Woodlanders saw dozens of zoo workers outside. Jane and Harry were there with guns.

Mrs. Tandy asked quietly, "Is the lion dead?"

Chief Hemster said, "They just shot him with something to quiet him down. I bet he will be up in twenty minutes."

Jane and Harry and the others loaded the huge animal into a truck. They drove it back to the lion house.

Chief Hemster and the Woodlanders went outside and sat on the steps of the bird house.

Bill said, "Wow! I was sure scared."

Dave said, "I was, too."

Kathy said, "But, Dave! You told me

not to worry. So I thought I was the only one who was scared."

Mrs. Tandy said, "I was so scared I almost fainted!"

Sammy said, "I would have fainted but I don't know how.

"I just kept hoping the lion wasn't as hungry as I am!"

Then they saw Jane and Harry. They were in a big hurry.

Mrs. Tandy said, "Look, they're running to the monkey house!"

Bill said, "Let's get over there!"

By the time they got to the monkey house, Jane and Harry were running out of it.

Harry shouted, "Glad you folks are here! I can't believe this!"

Dave asked, "What's wrong?"

Harry answered, "Coco is missing!"

Jane said, "Will you help us find her?

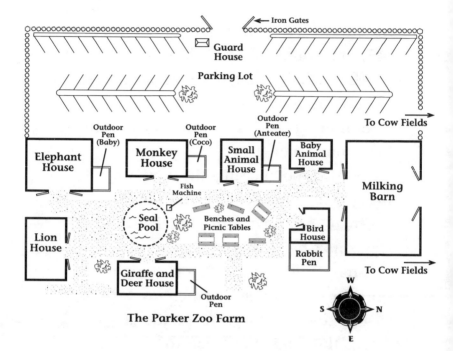

The Parker Zoo Farm

She's our new chimpanzee."

Sammy said, "We know her. In fact, she threw a peanut at me. Sure we will help you!"

Bill said, "Dave, you come with me. Spread out, everybody!"

40

Jane called, "Let's meet at the baby-animal house in fifteen minutes."

But when they got together again, no one had seen Coco.

Harry said, "We've asked every zoo worker. No luck."

Jane said, "But did you see how strange the new worker acted when we asked him?

"He said he wouldn't answer dumb questions. Then he stomped off."

Harry said, "I don't know what that guy's problem is. Anyway, I called Tim Lopez about Coco. And I got word to the police, too."

Just then a mean-looking man raced up to them.

He shouted, "Some jerk broke into my car! You can't trust anybody around here!"

The front of his shirt was ripped open.

He waved his fist and ran off.

Sammy said, "Who was THAT?"

Harry said, "Our new worker, Fred Sly."

Chief Hemster joked, "Happy fellow!"

Bill said, "I wonder why he was out by his car when everyone else was out looking for Coco."

Dave said, "Good question. Let's head over to Coco's cage and look around for clues."

They headed for the monkey house.

Mrs. Tandy took one look inside and pointed to the floor. She said, "There are two buttons lying there!"

Kathy said, "Remember how torn up Fred Sly's shirt looked? Do you think they're his?"

Just then another zoo worker came running in. He was out of breath.

He said, "You're not going to believe this. I hardly believe it myself ... Baby is gone, too!"

Sammy said, "Oh, come on. How could someone steal an elephant?"

They raced to the elephant house.

■   ■   ■

As they ran, not one of them saw an old blue truck pull slowly out of the iron gate at the back of the zoo.

Chapter 6:
The Blue Truck

Kathy found the first clue ... in Baby's pen.

Dave said, "Hey, Kathy, that's the end part of a cane!"

Chief Hemster looked around on the floor outside the pen. He said, "Here's a trail of hay, from here to the back door!"

Sammy said, "I can understand how someone could steal a chimp. They're not that big.

"But I STILL don't see how anybody could steal Baby.

"You can't exactly sneak around with an elephant!"

Dave said, "Well, someone could have driven up to the elephant-house door ... and just led him into a truck."

Bill added, "That would at least explain why the trail of hay ends right outside the door."

Harry said, "Baby's very old, and he doesn't like strangers. I'm surprised he'd let anyone lead him anywhere."

Jane said, "I was thinking the same thing."

Sammy said, "Then the crooks must have had a bunch of people to push him and pull him ... and hold food out to him ... to get him to go into the truck."

Harry said, "Well, Jane and I have to go check on the other animals. We will get back to you as soon as we can!"

By this time, Chief Jordan had arrived from Parker's police station.

Tim Lopez, the zoo owner, had flown in by helicopter.

They were talking outside the elephant house when the Woodlanders came out with Chief Hemster.

Chief Hemster said, "Nothing much yet to report ... I'll fill you in as we walk. Let's go find out if any one saw a strange truck come into the zoo."

They all went to talk to the guard at the delivery gate.

She said, "I saw only one strange truck ... a few minutes after the lion scare this morning.

"The old man said he was here to deliver hay to the elephant house."

Chief Jordan asked, "What did the truck look like?"

The guard said, "It was old, but it was painted bright blue.

"It had back doors and a big side door. The windows were painted over to look like curtains."

Dave asked, "Did you see the license plates? Do you remember even ONE letter or number?"

The guard said, "I sure do. It was all letters, no numbers. It said I-M-BAY-B."

She walked over to a book inside the gate house. She said, "Here it is. I write all the license numbers down."

She pointed to her book. It said, "10:34 A.M. Blue truck. Illinois license plate: I-M-BAY-B."

Chief Jordan said, "I'll send this license number out to the other police officers."

He ran over to his car and back.

Mr. Lopez said, "Would my helicopter be of any use? We could look for the truck from the air."

Chief Hemster said, "Fine idea! It would be a fast way to check the big roads. How many people does it hold?"

Mr. Lopez answered, "Up to six people and the pilot."

Sammy cried, "Hey, Chief Hemster, there's room for you AND all of us!"

Chief Jordan said, "Great! We have to find that truck.

"I'll stay here and look for more clues. I'll get Harry and Jane to help me out. Let's meet at twelve thirty."

Mr. Lopez said, "I'll pick everyone up at the helicopter field."

"After you're back, we can have lunch and talk."

The helicopter took off, making its loud CHOP-CHOP-CHOP noise.

They rose up into the air.

Sammy shouted, "Hey! I forgot something. Let me off!"

Kathy shouted, "What did you forget?"

Sammy shouted, "I forgot I might be SCARED!"

Dave shouted, "Too late to get out! Look how far up we are!"

Mrs. Tandy opened her shopping bag. She said, "Maybe something in here will keep your mind off the ride, honey."

Sammy leaned over and looked inside the bag. He pulled out some big red apples and a huge bag of corn chips.

They all started munching.

Sammy shouted, "I feel better already! Look at the zoo farm from here!"

He pointed with his apple. "The cows look about as big as cats."

He munched on some corn chips.

Bill said, "Hey, wait a minute! What will a blue truck look like from up here?"

Chief Hemster said, "Probably like a little blue lunch box on wheels."

51

They dipped down over every road and parking lot, looking for the truck. They even flew over Bluff Lake.

They saw trees, houses, garages, cars, vans, schools, stores, trains, tracks, rivers, lakes, factories, buses, and tractors.

But they didn't see a blue truck.

At last Chief Hemster told the pilot to go back to the zoo farm.

Chapter 7:
A Good Guy or a Crook?

As the helicopter landed, Kathy said, "That was sure fun. But we didn't get much done."

Mrs. Tandy said, "Well, we did one

good thing. We made my shopping bag easier to carry!"

As they got out, Mr. Lopez came running up with Chief Jordan, Jane, and Harry. They were all waving wildly.

Mr. Lopez shouted, "We have some news! A phone call came in for Harry ... about Coco and Baby!"

Chief Hemster asked, "What kind of phone call?"

Harry said, "Well, it was a man's voice. He said that Coco and Baby were fine. He said we'd have them back in three days."

Chief Jordan said, "Then whoever it was hung up."

Mr. Lopez said, "Well, let's have lunch, everybody. We can talk about this then."

They all went to a restaurant near the zoo farm.

After a few minutes Sammy said, "This

fried chicken is great! Now my brain is working."

Mr. Lopez said, "What does it come up with, my boy?"

Sammy said, "It comes up with a question. Is the man who phoned Harry a good guy or a crook?"

Chief Jordan said, "That's a good question. If he's a crook, why would he call to say the animals were safe?"

Chief Hemster said, "And if he's a good guy, why did he take Coco and Baby in the first place?"

55

Bill said, "Could it be some sort of weirdo who phoned? Maybe he didn't even take the missing animals."

Kathy asked, "Then how would he know about them?"

Dave said, "Chief Jordan, tell us what you found out while we were gone."

He said, "The fact is, all zoo visitors said they were indoors while the lion was loose."

Bill said, "Were any of them in the elephant house?"

Chief Jordan nodded. "Yes, but no one saw anything strange."

Kathy asked, "How about the monkey house?"

Mr. Lopez said, "The visitors couldn't get into it. It was locked up tight."

Harry said, "So it must have been an inside job.

"Someone with a zoo key locked that door.

"People had to run to other places to get away from the lion."

Sammy cried, "What a rat! He didn't care if those people got eaten! He just wanted to steal animals!"

Mrs. Tandy said, "Well, a person who would lock people outside with a lion wouldn't call to tell us Coco and Baby are safe.

57

"I think we must be dealing with two people."

Mr. Lopez said, "I believe you're right, Becky Tandy!"

Chief Hemster said, "Did you find out where all the zoo workers were when the lion was loose?"

Chief Jordan said, "Every worker remembered seeing one or two others. It turned out that every single worker was there."

Jane said, "Even the new guy?"

Chief Jordan shook his head. "Well, no one remembered seeing Fred Sly until later on, when the lion was waking up."

Sammy said, "So what do we do next? We can't just sit and hope Coco and Baby come back."

Mr. Lopez said, "The circus Coco and Baby used to be in is coming to Bluff Lake later today.

"I'm going to fly there and talk with the owner. She may know something about this.

"Will you meet me there in Bluff Lake around four o'clock, after I talk with her?"

Dave said, "Sure! We will see you then!"

The Woodlanders went back to the zoo farm to get their car.

They drove back to Bluff Lake and into their driveway.

■   ■   ■

But they didn't see what was parked right around the corner, next to their woods.

It was a blue truck.

Chapter 8:
Surprise Company

Mrs. Tandy said, "Well, this has been quite a day."

Sammy said, "You know it! And I was just trying to get rid of Jumper."

Kathy said, "That's right ... you never did tell Harry and Jane about Jumper!"

Sammy said, "Oh, yeah. Too bad."

Dave said, "What if we go finish making the bookshelf for the clubhouse ... before we go to the circus tonight?"

Bill said, "Good idea. Here, I'll put Mop out on his leash."

But Mop started barking the minute he got outside. His little tan legs raced back and forth across the yard.

Kathy said, "Quiet, Mop!" She patted his head. "Everything's OK."

But Mop kept on running and jumping and barking. They had to put him back inside.

The Woodlanders' clubhouse stood on the back lawn near the woods. It was the size of a small garage, but it looked like a real house.

They all started in on the bookshelf.

Kathy sawed one shelf board. Sammy sawed another.

Bill and Dave were sanding.

Mrs. Tandy hammered three large nails into one side of the bookcase to hold up the first shelf.

She said, "Uh-oh. We've used up almost all the big nails."

Sammy said, "I'll ride over to the hardware store and get some more."

He ran over to his bike. He started wheeling it to the sidewalk.

Suddenly he came to a stop at the edge of the woods.

He dropped his bike down with a bang.

He said to himself, "Holy cow! No wonder Mop was barking! Am I seeing things or did I just see an elephant?"

He looked hard at a hole in the bushes.

Nothing was there.

He thought, "I must've been at the zoo too long. I'm going animal crazy."

He bent over to pick up his bike.

He heard a branch snap.

He looked up slowly, without making any sudden moves ... right into the face of a pygmy elephant!

He whispered, "You must be Baby! What are YOU doing here?"

Slowly he put out his hand.

The elephant put its trunk into

Sammy's hand and poked around, searching for peanuts.

Sammy said, "Come on, boy." He took hold of the trunk and tried to pull Baby onto the lawn.

But the elephant only pulled back into the dark woods.

Sammy tip-toed back to the clubhouse.

Bill said, "My gosh, Sammy! What's wrong? Why do you have that weird look on your face?"

Sammy said, "When I tell you, you're not going to believe me. Baby is in our woods."

Bill said, "Yeah, right."

But when he took another look at Sammy he said, "Hey, you're not joking! Baby's out there?"

Sammy led them all right to the spot where he had seen Baby.

Dave whispered, "If he's still here, we

should try to get him into the garage."

Mrs. Tandy said softly, "I'll run over there and drive the station wagon onto the street. I'll leave the garage door wide open."

Kathy said, "I'll run in and get some food. Maybe then he will follow us."

She hurried back with a big plate of oatmeal cookies.

Sammy picked up a cookie and said, "Be really quiet."

Then he yelled, "YOW! HOLY SMOKE!"

An elephant trunk had reached out of the woods and grabbed the oatmeal cookie from his hand!

Bill whispered, "Hey! Walk around the house, Sammy, to the garage."

"Follow us," Kathy added. "We will keep handing you cookies."

Dave said, "I'll come last. My chair makes a lot of noise on the path. I don't want to scare him."

Sammy fed cookies to Baby, one after another.

Baby walked all the way out of the woods and onto the path. He followed Sammy like a friendly dog.

First Bill, then Mrs. Tandy, then Kathy, then Sammy and Baby, then Dave, paraded into the garage.

Mrs. Tandy closed the garage door, and they all stood around Baby, petting him.

Bill said, "Let's give him some water and something to eat besides cookies."

Sammy said, "Why would he want anything besides cookies?"

He jammed one into his mouth. He added, "But I'll bring him something else."

Then he ran into the kitchen.

Bill said, "I'll stay out here in the garage with Baby.

"Why don't you guys get the clubhouse cleared up ... and Dave, you can call Mr. Lopez and Chief Hemster."

Sammy showed up with two buckets of water and some carrots.

Mrs. Tandy said, "Sammy, since you and Baby have eaten all the cookies, why don't you and I make more for Mr. Lopez?"

Sammy said, "Cookies for Mr. Lopez!" They walked into the kitchen.

He teased, "Chief Hemster isn't going to like this at all! Mrs. T. has a new bo-o-y friend, Mrs. T. has a—"

Laughing, Mrs. Tandy grabbed a cracker and popped it into his mouth.

She said, "Shh ... you little parrot! Now help me mix these cookies!"

As they mixed, Dave came into the kitchen to help.

Soon they had the new batch of cookies out of the oven.

Just then Kathy walked in the back
door.   She was leading a new friend by
the hand.

She said, "Look who came walking
into the clubhouse!   She pulled on the
back of my shirt.

"When I turned around and saw her I
nearly died!"

It was Coco!

The others crowded around her.   Mrs.
Tandy said, "What are we running here,
a zoo?   An elephant in the garage and a
chimpanzee in the kitchen!"

Mop ran in and sniffed Coco's feet.
Coco walked up to Sammy and took his
hand.

Then she jumped onto Dave's lap.
She saw the plate of cookies on the table.
She took a cookie in each hand and

stuffed them both into her mouth.

Mrs. Tandy said, "Look! She eats cookies Sammy-style!

"Well, we are NOT going to lose another batch of cookies."

She picked up the plate and slipped it into the oven. She said, "These are for HUMAN guests."

Just then they heard a knock on the door.

Chapter 9:
The Stranger

Sammy said, "This time it's probably the lion!

"Tell him HE can't have our cookies, either!

"Tell him to go home!"

Kathy went to the door. She called, "Who is it?"

A man's voice answered, "You don't know me. I'm here to explain about Coco and Baby."

Coco began clapping her long, dark, glove-like hands.

She jumped off Dave's lap and, with a funny rocking walk, went to the door.

She tried to pull it open.

But she couldn't.

So she got mad! She let out a scream and kicked the door.

Then she took Kathy's hand and put it on the doorknob.

Kathy laughed. "Well, it looks like Coco knows the person outside."

Dave wheeled over to the window to look out.

He said, "I saw that guy at the zoo.

74

Let's trust Coco, and let him in."

Kathy opened the door.

There stood a bent, gray-haired man with a cane.

Dave noticed that the rubber tip of his cane was missing!

The man put his cane down.

Then he stood up straight!

He smiled when Coco ran up to him and began to hug his knees.

All of a sudden he didn't look old at all.

He said, "I'm Sid McBay. I'm a retired circus detective and clown. And I have a lot to tell you."

Dave said, "Can you hold on a second, Mr. McBay? Bill will want to hear this, and he's out in the garage with Baby."

Mr. McBay said, "Fine, fine. Shall we go see Baby, Coco?"

He made a loop with his arms and Coco climbed right up, and onto his back.

They went to the garage.

Bill was sitting on a box. He was scratching Baby's belly.

Baby was swaying from side to side with something like a smile on his face.

When he saw Mr. McBay, he raised his trunk in the air. Then he made a sound like a brass horn.

Bill gasped when he saw Coco hugging the stranger.

He said, "Who are you?"

Mrs. Tandy said, "Come into the house and we will all find out."

Just then they heard a car drive up. It was Chief Hemster and Mr. Lopez.

Chief Hemster said, "Tim here flew over to the Bluff Lake circus grounds, and I picked him up there."

Mr. McBay shook hands with Mr. Lopez and Chief Hemster.

He said, "I'm so glad to meet you.

"I was just about to tell everyone about Coco and Baby.

"Won't you two sit down?"

Mr. McBay cleared his throat.

He began, "I used to work for the circus that's in town now.

"Thirty-eight years ago, when I was just twenty, I joined that circus as a clown. I trained myself to be a circus detective, too.

"I trained Baby and made up my clown act around him. 'McBay and Baby' we were called.

"Baby rode in my blue truck in our act. The license plates are I-M-BAY-B, you know."

Dave said, "Oh, NOW I get it! It reads 'I am Baby!'"

Bill said, "No wonder he was glad to see you. You're like Baby's family!"

Mr. McBay said, "Yes. And Baby is why I left the circus. I'm still going strong, but Baby got sick every time we moved to a new town.

"The circus decided to sell him ... and Coco. I wanted to stay near them.

"I hoped to get a job with your zoo farm, Mr. Lopez."

Mr. Lopez asked, "Then why didn't you

come to see me right away?"

Mr. McBay said, "Because the day be-fore I left the zoo, I over-heard some people planning to steal Coco and Baby.

"I was outside a tent. Three men in-side it were talking."

Chief Hemster asked, "Did you know their voices?"

Mr. McBay said, "Only one, the loud-est one. The meanest, most big-mouthed young man I ever heard ... your new zoo worker, Fred Sly."

Mr. Lopez said, "You mean he got a

job with us just to steal the animals?"

Mr. McBay said, "Yes, I'm afraid so. And I knew they were going to steal them, but not WHEN.

"So every day I've come to the zoo to keep an eye on Sly."

Kathy said, "But what if he saw you there?"

Mr. McBay said, "My dear, he'd never know who I was.

"I made myself up to look like a different person every day.

"One day I was a bent old man with a beard.

"Another day a sea captain.

"Any way, now I'm trying to find out who the other two animal thieves are besides Sly.

"All I know about them is that they work for the circus. And they're in town now.

"We had six animals stolen from the circus last year, and now those crooks are starting on the zoo. But this time I'm going to catch them!"

Sammy said, "But why did YOU steal Baby and Coco?"

Bill poked him in the ribs.

Mr. McBay said, "I didn't steal Coco. Fred Sly did.

"He let the lion loose, and then took Coco. He hid her in a laundry bag in his car, in the parking lot.

"My truck was in the parking lot, too. I watched Sly leave his car.

"So I put Coco in my truck. Then I drove around to the back gate to get Baby.

"I knew they were planning to grab him right after they stole Coco.

"So I took him first, to protect him."

Bill said, "But why did you bring the

animals to us?"

Mr. McBay said, "Yesterday, at the zoo, I listened to you talk.

"I could tell you were people I could trust. I could see that you love animals.

"And I heard you say you live in the woods. You had everything I needed to save Coco and Baby."

Mrs. Tandy asked, "Why didn't you tell all this to Jane or Harry?"

Mr. McBay said, "What if they were in with the thieves? I was afraid to tell them."

Mr. Lopez said, "Well, you've done the zoo a big favor, Mr. McBay."

Chief Hemster said, "And you've helped the police quite a bit, too!"

Sammy said, "Hey, now I see why you didn't need any help loading Baby into the truck. I bet he would follow you anywhere."

Mr. McBay said, "Right. I'm sorry he broke his leg rope. I hope he didn't stomp on anything in your woods."

Kathy said, "I'm sure it's OK. Hey, wait a minute! Are you the one who saved Peewee when the big gorilla hurt her?"

Mr. McBay nodded.

Sammy said, "So I bet it was you who took care of the cow and the new calf born in the field!"

Mr. McBay nodded again.

Bill added, "And was it you who

found some animal cages un-locked one night at the zoo?

"Are you the one who flashed a warning light?"

Mr. McBay said, "Yes, I was!"

He looked at his watch. "But I better not talk much longer. I have to get to the circus now.

"Part of the thieves' plan was to take one of the circus tigers, too. Maybe they'll still try it, who knows."

Dave said, "Mr. McBay, we want to help you find these crooks."

Mr. McBay said, "That's a fine idea!"

"I can use your help, if it's all right with the circus owner.

"Let's go find out!"

Chapter 10: The Five New Clowns

They piled into the blue truck and drove to the circus.

Chief Hemster and Mr. Lopez followed them in the police car.

They met Rosa Gump, the circus owner. She said, "I do need help. But how could you help me?

"How could five new people snoop around without the crooks catching on?"

Everyone stood thinking. Then Mr. McBay said to Mrs. Gump, "Boss, let's talk for a minute."

They walked away.

When they came back, Mrs. Gump had a big grin on her face.

She said, "Becky. Kids. How'd you like to meet my brand-new weekend clown act?"

Sammy shouted, "Sure! Where are they? Who are they?"

Mrs. Gump said, "They're right here!

"There are five of them!

"They're called 'The Woodland Clowns.'

"YOU are the new act!"

Sammy asked, "Do you mean to say

you'd let us be clowns for three days?"

Mrs. Gump said, "Let you! I'm BEG-
GING you to. Will you do it?"

Sammy jumped into the air.

He shouted, "Yipee! Peanut Hair, the
Nutty Clown, is READY!"

Chief Hemster laughed. He said, "This
I've got to see! And maybe I will!

"I'm on duty here at the circus this
whole weekend. So I'll see you around!"

He and Mr. Lopez left to explore the
grounds.

Mrs. Gump said, "So who's going to
be what?"

Bill said, "I've always wanted to wear
big fat clown shoes."

Mrs. Tandy said, "I'm so thin and tall,
I'd like to make myself look even taller."

Dave said, "I'd like to fix up my chair
to look like a train!"

Kathy said, "I think I'd like to be a

shy, scared clown.

"That way, if I really am scared, they'll think it's part of the act!"

Mrs. Gump said, "Come with me, clowns. First stop, costume tent."

They stepped inside a big tent. There were clown clothes everywhere.

There were floppy pants.

One pair had one red leg and one green one.

Some were striped.

Some had big flowers on them.

There were skinny pants, too.

Mrs. Tandy chose a pair of those, black and shiny.

She chose big clown shoes with four-inch-thick soles.

She chose a tall black hat. The top was almost torn off, and stood straight up.

Then she found a white T-shirt, and a fancy blue suit jacket.

Dave said, "You look like you had a stork mother and a penguin father. It's great!"

Sammy, Bill, and a circus worker had already put a cardboard engine together to fit over Dave's wheelchair.

Now the man was painting it black with spray paint.

Dave had a blue-and-white-striped hat, and a jacket to match. He had on a pair of huge rubber ears. "So I can hear other trains," he said.

He had a rubber horn to let the other clowns know he was coming.

He even had a fake smoke-maker, to make smoke come out of the train.

Kathy pulled out a yellow-and-black-striped shirt and huge floppy shoes. She painted her face white.

She took the pants that were half-red, half-green.

She said, "Dave, how's this?

"When I wave my red leg at you, you have to slow down and stop. If you don't, I'll pretend to faint.

"When I have my arms out, it will mean the other clowns have to wait … because the train's coming."

Bill added, "The rest of us can almost get run over. Then we can jump away."

Sammy said, "If we other clowns get

mad, we can take a bucket of tiny paper scraps that look like water ... and throw them at each other!"

Dave said, "Maybe when we grow up we should ALL be clowns!"

Mr. McBay and Mrs. Gump smiled at each other.

Sammy said, "Look, I have my wig ready!" He had found a curly yellow one, and tied peanuts all over it.

He really was Peanut Hair!

He put on some giant gloves, a fake nose, and big fake glasses with black rims.

Bill said, "You look wild! If I didn't know you, I'd start running and never come back!"

Dave asked, "Where's YOUR costume, Bill?"

Bill said, "Wait a minute."

He ran behind a big box. He said, "I'm putting it on now, and here I come!"

Out ran a big yellow duck with an orange bill.

It gave a loud quack, and chased after Sammy.

Mr. McBay said, "You all picked great costumes! Let's try out your acts in a circus ring!

"You'll have plenty of time."

Mrs. Tandy said, "Perfect! This way the crooks will get used to us being around, and we can start our snooping."

The circus workers were finishing up

the tent.

The seats and lights were all in place.

The cages for the wild animals were in the middle ring.

The rings and bars for the acrobats were ready. The net was in place, too.

Mr. McBay said, "This is just how it will be for the show ... except with people watching you!"

Dave said, "I think they'd like us more if we move around as one bunch of clowns. They'd see us better."

So they tried out their act.

Other circus workers came over to watch them.

They were wild.

They were silly.

They were FUNNY!

At last Mr. McBay said, "OK, it's six o'clock. You'd better get home for dinner. But be back by eight thirty for the show."

Mrs. Tandy asked, "Won't you eat with us, Sid? And stay for the weekend?"

Dave whispered to Mr. McBay, "That way you can keep track of Baby and Coco, right in our garage."

Kathy whispered, "And Mrs. T. and I can get carrots for Baby from the grocery store!"

Bill whispered, "And we can help you clean up the garage after them."

But Sammy only said, "Yuck!"

Mr. McBay laughed. "How can I say no to all that?"

Chapter 11:
The Dark Circus Tent

Mrs. Tandy said, "Well, it's just about two hours until the show. Let's just leave our costumes on."

Bill said, "I'll get the clothes we left in the tent.

"Load Dave's engine into the truck, guys."

Bill ran over to the costume tent. It was almost dark inside.

He got all their clothes. He bent down in back of a big box to find his shoes.

He was still behind the box when he heard a voice say, "We will take the tiger, anyway. Sometime this weekend."

Another voice said, "Nothing better

ruin our plans this time, Sly."

THE CROOKS!

Bill was too scared to move.

If they saw him, they might hurt him. Besides, he had to hear their plans.

He froze where he was.

One of the men came near the box Bill was hiding behind.

The man leaned against it as he sat on a smaller one.

Bill could see the man's head from the back.

He had blond, curly hair under his army cap. His neck was thick and red.

A very deep voice said, "We've got a big truck. Why not pick out some other animals now that the chimp and the elephant are gone?"

The blond man said, "Sneak around tonight, Sly. See which ones we can steal, OK?"

Just then Bill heard footsteps coming toward the tent.

Then he heard the three men running out.

Next he heard somebody walking toward him, inside the tent.

A voice said softly, "Bill, where are you? Are you in here? I came back to help carry stuff."

It was Sammy!

Bill tip-toed out from behind the box and whispered, "I'm here, Sammy, but act like I'm not.

"I'll tell you why later.

"Go around in back of the tent and make sure no one's watching it. If it's safe for me to come out, give our secret whistle.

"Then run to the truck, FAST. I'll slide out from under the tent and follow you there."

Sammy whispered, "OK."

In a minute Bill heard Sammy's secret whistle.

He crawled out from the tent and stood up in the dark, holding tight to the clothes in his arms.

He headed toward the parking lot.

In a flash someone jumped in front of him and grabbed him.

A deep voice said, "Gotcha, you little sneak! What are you doing walking between the tents? Get out in the light so I can see who you are!"

Bill was more scared than he had been in his whole life.

So he kicked like a mule! He got the man right in the shin!

The man's shout echoed across the circus grounds.

"O–W–W–W–W!"

He let go of Bill.

Bill ran all the way to the truck. He got there just behind Sammy.

He whispered to Sammy, "Get in, NOW."

They jumped in, and Bill sank to the floor on top of the heap of clothes he was carrying.

He said, "Let's get out of here, Mr. McBay! And fast! They're after me!"

Chapter 12:
The Clowns at Work

On the way back to Bluff Lake, Bill told them what had happened.

Mr. McBay said, "That man you kicked ... do you think he knew who you were? Did he know you were in the tent?"

Bill shook his head. "No. I don't think so.

"He doesn't even know it was Sammy who came into the tent after me.

"All three of those guys just ran away when they heard his footsteps.

"It was really lucky Sammy whispered instead of shouting when he came inside."

Sammy shouted, "LUCK! That wasn't LUCK! Those were BRAINS at work! Detectives don't shout!"

Kathy laughed. "You're shouting right now, Mr. Detective!"

Sammy said, "Sure! But right now I'm a brother, not a detective."

To prove it, he put the duck mask over Bill's head.

Then he pushed his face into it.

He gave Bill a big noisy kiss, right on

the duck bill.

Everyone laughed.

Dave said, "Hey! Put that in the clown act!"

Then Bill stretched up his neck and came down with his rubber bill ... WHACK ... right on Sammy's head.

Mrs. Tandy laughed. She said, "Put that in, too!"

As they made dinner, they talked over their plans.

Mr. McBay said, "Well, there are two

men at the circus who have VERY deep voices.

"In fact, they call one of them FROGGY, his voice is so low. He's a tent worker. I wonder if he's the one."

Bill said, "Once we find Deep-voice and Blond-man, we can watch for them both.

"Then we can go after them."

Dave asked, "Who's the other man with a deep voice, Mr. McBay?"

He answered, "He's the man who helps Rosa Gump run the circus. His name is Mack, Richard Mack.

"But he's paid a lot for his work. I doubt he'd risk his job by stealing animals."

After dinner, Kathy said, "Well, it's time to get back to the circus. Now's our chance to be clowns! I'm a little scared ... but it'll be fun."

And it was fun!

They were the hit of the show.

After the show, Kathy went back to the costume tent. She wanted a bigger hat to wear for the next day's act.

Two men walked in. One was Fred Sly. The other was wearing a suit and a bowtie. He sat down on a box near the tent door.

Sly said, "Wait a minute! Look, there's someone here. We can't talk."

The other man said, in a deep bull-frog voice, "I'm sure the pretty little clown won't mind leaving."

He looked hard at Kathy. He said, "We need this tent to talk."

Kathy knew from his deep voice and suit that he must be Rosa Gump's partner, Mr. Mack.

And she knew she had to find out what they were talking about.

She went outside.   It was dark, and she was scared.

But she hid in the deep grass outside the tent to listen.

She heard Mr. Mack's voice.   He said, "We will do the job tomorrow night.   Tell your friend to come then.

"I'll see you both right after the show starts.   Which animals are we taking besides the tiger?"

Fred Sly said, "The ostrich, the bears, and the seal. I've got it all planned out. They're near each other."

Mr. Mack said, "Be sure you're on time. This HAS to work. I need money! I've been gambling and I owe everyone in town."

Then they left the tent. They didn't see Kathy outside in the night, almost afraid to breathe.

Kathy got up and tip-toed back to tell the others what she had heard.

Mr. McBay said, "Fine work, Kathy. Now we know for sure they're not doing it until tomorrow night."

Dave said, "And we know Mr. Mack is in on it."

Sammy said, "And we know what animals they're taking. The tiger, the ostrich, the bears, and a seal."

Mr. McBay said, "Tomorrow night I'll have to guard the cages."

Dave said, "Well, it looks like the Woodland Clowns will miss the Saturday night show!

"We want to be free to help watch the cages with you."

Mr. McBay said, "Good! I'll need you! Dave and Sammy, tomorrow night you keep watch near the seal.

"Bill and Kathy, you stay near the ostriches.

"Becky, you and I can keep an eye on the bears."

When they got home, Chief Hemster was waiting there for them.

They told him about their plan.

He said, "Tomorrow night I'll hide out at the cages, too. With Rosa Gump. And Chief Jordan. And Mr. Lopez, if he's willing.

"We can all use two-way radios, and I'll have officers in patrol cars standing by."

Sammy said, "Well, we have a good plan here, except for one thing."

Chief Hemster asked, "What's that?"

Sammy said, "Saturday night everyone will miss the best clown act in America!"

He socked Bill and ran off to bed.

Chapter 13:
The Show's Over!

The Woodland Clowns were a big hit the next day at the afternoon show.

When it was over, they ate dinner at the circus.

They had hot dogs, peanuts, ice cream, and cotton candy.

Then they kept an eye on the circus animals until it was time for the night show.

Finally, the parade began.

First the elephants walked in. They wore blankets of red, blue, gold, and purple.

They stopped walking and stood on their hind legs.

Then each one turned in a circle, and began to walk again.

Next came the wild animals in their golden cages.

Twenty dogs in little skirts and fluffy collars hopped along in a row.

White horses trotted after them.

Then tight-rope walkers in shiny yellow costumes danced past.

And last came some clowns, jumping

and fooling around as they marched.

But the Woodland Clowns were missing.

They were hiding near the animal cages back by the circus tents. With them were Rosa Gump, the two police chiefs, and Mr. Lopez.

An old woman with white hair, a cane, and a big purse, was walking near the·cages under a light.

It was good old Mr. McBay, in costume again.

After fifteen minutes of hiding near the ostriches, Bill whispered to Kathy, "It looks like the crooks aren't showing up."

Kathy said, "I'm starting to worry, too. Maybe they changed their plans."

But just then they heard an engine.

The noise grew louder as a huge truck backed up to the bear cage.

Its lights were off. Three men jumped out of it.

One of them said, "I don't believe this. There's an old lady near the cage."

The man who spoke was wearing an army cap.

Then a deep voice said, "What are you doing, snooping around here, lady! This area is off limits to you!"

It was Mr. Mack.

He said, "Get the old bat out of here, Sly."

The old woman said, "Don't be rude to me, young man. I'll go by myself. Leave me alone."

Then she called to the bears, "Good-bye, you darling animals!"

She limped off into the darkness ... and hid right behind the bear cage.

Fred Sly, Mr. Mack, and the man in the cap slid a wide board partly out of the truck. They slid it under the bear-cage door.

Sly said, "Let's get the small bear onto the ramp first. The bigger one may follow her."

Mr. Mack said, "Man, that big one is REALLY big! We can get a lot of money for him."

They opened the bear-cage door.

Then all three men started using poles to poke at the smaller bear.

Mr. Mack said, "She's beginning to move. Poke her again!"

But another voice boomed out, "You three! Freeze! Police!"

It was Chief Hemster.

Sly shouted, "Make a break for it!" The three ran off through the darkness.

Rosa Gump slammed the bear-cage door shut.

Sly ran behind the cage.

A clown with very long legs tripped him. An old lady threw down her cane and pinned him down.

Chief Jordan said, "Great work, you two." He read Fred Sly his rights and clamped him into handcuffs.

The curly-haired man ran in back of the seal cage. But something that felt like a bag of cement stood in his way.

It was Sammy!

The man gasped. "Oof!"

Then Dave pushed him to the ground.

"Got him!" called Chief Hemster.

Mr. Mack had run behind the ostrich cage.

Bill tackled his knees. Kathy sat down on his legs. Mr. Lopez held him down.

Chief Jordan, with Sly in hand, got handcuffs onto him.

A minute later a police car drove up.

A police officer began taking snapshots of the truck, the poles, and the ramp to the bears' cage.

She took pictures of the men in handcuffs, the bears, the clowns, the police officers, and everyone else around.

117

Sammy said, "Wow! That will make a whole book about catching the crooks!"

Mr. Lopez said, "Yes, and it will help put them in jail."

Finally Rosa Gump said, "Tonight's circus is only half over.

"I have to get back to look after everything. But I sure wish the Woodland Clowns would stay on until we leave town tomorrow."

Sammy said, "We WILL!

"We LOVE it!

"In fact, let's get back to the ring right now!"

Mrs. Tandy said, "And let's all meet back at our house after the show for a party. What do you say?"

Sammy cried, "Hot dog!"

Bill said, "Let's phone Harry and Jane to come."

And that's just what they did.

Back home, the Woodlanders sat in their circus costumes and ate oatmeal cookies and ice cream.

At the party Mr. Lopez gave Mr. McBay the job of detective for the Parker Zoo Farm.

Rosa Gump asked the Woodlanders if they would do their clown act every year, when her circus came to town.

They said yes, of course.

Everyone had fun at the party, even Mop. He lay on his back, dreaming of elephants in his woods.

Jane said, "Every mystery has been solved, except for one."

Dave asked, "What's that?"

She said, "Harry and I still can't figure out how a beautiful big black rabbit got into our pen of gray rabbits."

Sammy tried not to laugh.

He snorted instead ... and milk

119

bubbled out of his nose!

Then everyone began to laugh.

And somehow, in the excitement, Sammy never did answer Jane's question about a mysterious black rabbit.